THE SPOOKY KISS. . . .

Bump! Bump! Bump!
It was coming closer and CLOSER.
SMACK!
Something wet touched Dudley's beak.

Dudley screamed and jumped
right out of his slippers.
He ran back to his bedroom,
slammed the door shut, and locked it.
He jumped into bed and pulled the covers
over his head.

"This is a fine how-do-you-do!" said Dudley.
"My lovely house is *haunted*!"

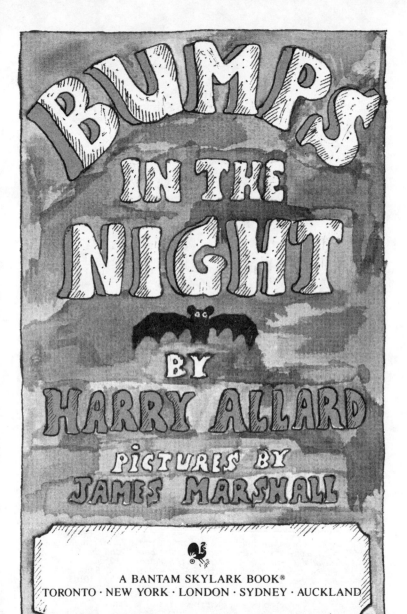

BUMPS
IN THE
NIGHT

BY
HARRY ALLARD

PICTURES BY
JAMES MARSHALL

A BANTAM SKYLARK BOOK®
TORONTO · NEW YORK · LONDON · SYDNEY · AUCKLAND

For my niece
Cathy Ann Dearolph
H.A.

For my nephew,
Alexander Christian Schwartz
J.M.

*This low-priced Bantam Book
has been completely reset in a type face
designed for easy reading, and was printed
from new plates. It contains the complete
text of the original hard-cover edition.*
NOT ONE WORD HAS BEEN OMITTED.

RL 4, 007–010

BUMPS IN THE NIGHT

*A Bantam Book / published by arrangement with
Doubleday and Company Inc.*

PRINTING HISTORY
Doubleday edition published September 1979

*Skylark Books is a registered trademark of Bantam Books, Inc.
Registered in the U.S. Patent and Trademark Office and
elsewhere.*

*Bantam Skylark edition / December 1984
6th printing through October 1987*

ISBN 0-553-15284-X

Published simultaneously in the United States and Canada

*Bantam Books are published by Bantam Books, Inc. Its trade-
mark, consisting of the words "Bantam Books" and the por-
trayal of a rooster, is Registered in U.S. Patent and Trademark
Office and in other countries. Marca Registrada. Bantam
Books, Inc., 666 Fifth Avenue, New York, New York 10103.*

PRINTED IN THE UNITED STATES OF AMERICA

CW   15   14   13   12   11   10   9   8   7   6

From ghoulics and ghosties
and three-leggety beasties,
And things that go
bump in the night,
Good Lord, deliver us.

Old Scottish Prayer

A SLEEPLESS NIGHT

Bong! Bong! Bong!
Bong! Bong! Bong!
Bong! Bong! Bong!
Bong! Bong! Bong!

The big grandfather clock in the hall
struck twelve: it was midnight.
But Dudley the Stork could not sleep.

He tossed and he turned.
He fluffed up his pillow.
He pulled his nightcap down over his ears.
He counted sheep.
He counted white sheep.
He counted black sheep.

1

Then he counted spotted sheep.
But it did not work.
Dudley still could not get to sleep.

Outside the wind was howling, howling,
and dark clouds covered the pale moon.

Wooosh! The big branches of an old elm tree
brushed against the side of Dudley's house.

Somewhere in the dark a hoot owl was hooting.
A shutter banged open and shut.
Windows rattled, floors creaked.

"What a night!" thought Dudley to himself.
Then, suddenly, Dudley heard *IT*.

Bump! Bump! Bump!

"What a strange noise!" said Dudley.
He turned on the light next to his bed.
He put on his glasses.
Bump! Bump! Bump!

"It is too loud for a mouse," said Dudley,
"but it is too soft for an elephant."
Bump! Bump! Bump!

The bumping sound seemed to be running
up and down the stairs.
Now it was in the dining room.
Now it was in the den.

Whatever it was turned the TV on,
then turned the TV off.
"Odd!" Dudley muttered to himself.

Dudley got out of bed.
Putting on his bathrobe and slippers,
he peeked out the bedroom door into the hall.

Bump! Bump! Bump!
The bumping sound was bumping
up the stairs again.

It was coming closer and CLOSER.

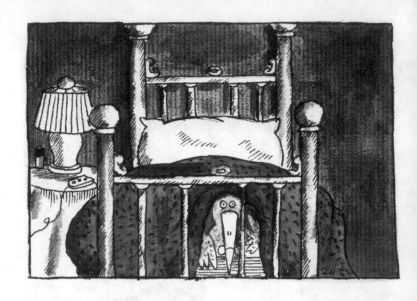

SMACK!
Something wet touched Dudley's beak.

Dudley screamed and jumped
right out of his slippers.
His glasses fell off.
He ran back to his bedroom,
slammed the door shut, and locked it.
He jumped into bed and pulled the covers
over his head.

Dudley the Stork could not believe what
he had seen—something big and white
running down the hall.

"This is a fine how-do-you-do!" said Dudley.
"My lovely house is *haunted*!"

TREVOR HOG
HAS AN IDEA

Early the next morning, Dudley called
his best friend, Trevor Hog.

"Dudley, you sound worried," Trevor said.
"Is anything wrong?"
"Yes, Trevor, something is wrong," said Dudley.
"My house is haunted. Things go bump in the
night, and something big and white ran down
the hall."

"It must have been a ghost," Trevor gulped.
"What can I do, Trevor?" Dudley asked.
Trevor thought. He thought hard.
He twitched his ears and wrinkled his nose.
"Hmm . . . hmm . . ." he hummed.

At last Trevor cleared his throat and said,
"Dudley, why don't you talk to the ghost
and find out what it wants?"

"Talk to a *ghost*?!" Dudley gasped.
"Why, I'd be too scared."

"But there are people who can talk to ghosts,"
Trevor said. "They are called mediums. A
medium acts as a go-between
between people and ghosts."
"Like a telephone operator?" asked Dudley.

"Exactly," said Trevor. "A medium puts you
through to ghosts . . . and other spooky things.
You must have a séance," Trevor continued.

"A *séance*?!" said Dudley.
"What on earth is a séance?"

"A séance," Trevor explained, "is when
a bunch of people sit around a table
at midnight with a medium."

"And what does the medium do?" asked Dudley.
"The medium asks you to hold hands," said Trevor.
"But why do you hold hands?" asked Dudley.
"Is it because your hands are cold?"
"No, Dudley," Trevor said.

"Is it because you are passing candy to one
another?" Dudley asked.
"No, Dudley," Trevor said.

"Is it because you are all in love?" Dudley asked.
"No, Dudley," Trevor said in a low voice.
"It's because you're all so *scared*,
that's why, Dudley."

Dudley the Stork gulped.
After a few seconds of silence, he asked,
"Do you know a good medium, Trevor?"

"Yes," Trevor half whispered, "I do."

CHAPTER THREE

A SPOOKY PAIR

There was a bad storm the next night—
thunder, lightning, and rain.
"What a night for a séance!" Dudley thought,
biting his nails.

Knock! Knock!
The guests were beginning to arrive.
Dudley went to the front door.
Trevor Hog and Grandpa Python had to hold up
Georgina the Ostrich because she was
shaking like a leaf.

Grandpa Python said he wasn't scared at all.
But he jumped a mile when Dagmar the Baboon
knocked over a vase.
Georgina the Ostrich started to cry.
Dagmar tried to make Georgina stop crying
and then started to cry herself.
Then Grandpa Python started to cry, too.

Aside from crying, no one said much.
They were all waiting for the medium.
They did not have long to wait.

At five minutes to midnight, a taxi
pulled up in front of Dudley's house.
There was a flash of lightning,
a clap of thunder, and a gust of wind.

A strange pair got out of the taxi.
It was the famous medium, Madam Kreepy,
and her helper, Lazlo Frog.

Lazlo was carrying a small black bag.
In it were Madam Kreepy's special hat . . .
and other things!

Dudley showed Madam Kreepy and Lazlo in.
"How do you do?" said Madam Kreepy
in a low, spooky voice.

Madam Kreepy shook hands with everyone.
Her hands were cold.

"Hello, Mrs. Creeper," said Grandpa Python.
"*Kreepy*," corrected Madam Kreepy.
"My name is Kreepy, not Creeper."

Then Madam Kreepy turned to Dudley
and asked, "Is everything ready?"
"Yes," said Dudley.

THE SÉANCE

Bong! Bong! Bong!
Bong! Bong! Bong!
Bong! Bong! Bong!
Bong! Bong! Bong!

Slowly, the big grandfather clock in the hall
struck twelve: it was midnight!
"It is time to start the séance,"
Madam Kreepy said softly.

Dudley the Stork showed Madam Kreepy and
Lazlo and his guests into the dining room.
Putting on her special hat, Madam Kreepy said,
"Please sit down and hold hands."
Madam Kreepy closed her eyes.

21

Boy, was it spooky too!

Georgina the Ostrich was so scared she had to
bite her lips to keep from screaming,
and Dagmar the Baboon was shaking like a leaf.
Trevor Hog broke out in a cold sweat.

Suddenly a gust of wind blew the candle out.
Dagmar and Grandpa dove under the table.
They hit their heads together.
The blow knocked Grandpa's false teeth
right out of his mouth!

Only Lazlo and Madam Kreepy remained calm.
"Please join hands again," she said.
And she closed her eyes again.

"Is Mrs. Creeper sleeping?" asked Grandpa.
"Shhh," said Dudley, putting his finger to his
beak. Madam Kreepy began to make gurgling
sounds in the back of her throat.
"Madam Kreepy is now in a trance," said Lazlo.

"Did you say Mrs. Creeper lost her pants?"
Grandpa Python asked in a loud whisper.
"No," said Lazlo. "I said Madam Kreepy was
in a deep *trance*."
"What's a t-t-trance?" asked Georgina.
"It's a deep sleep," explained Lazlo.
"But Madam Kreepy can still talk to us."

The famous medium was now in a deep,
deep trance.
She was, in fact, in the deepest trance
a spooky medium can be in.

CHAPTER FIVE

THE GHOST

"Ghost that is haunting this house,"
moaned Madam Kreepy.
"Ghost that is haunting this house,"
Madam Kreepy moaned louder.

"Madam Kreepy is trying to talk to the ghost,"
whispered Lazlo Frog.
"Show yourself now, now, NOW!" screamed
the medium.

"Is Mrs. Creeper feeling all right?" asked
Grandpa Python.
"Shhh . . ." everyone shushed Grandpa Python.
"Ghost, I command you to speak *now*!"
shrieked Madam Kreepy.

Suddenly, behind Madam Kreepy, the head
of a big white horse appeared.

"EEEK!!!" screamed Trevor Hog,
and fainted dead away.

Only Dudley the Stork kept his head.
"Who are you?" he asked the horse.

The horse grinned from ear to ear.
"Allow me to introduce myself," he
answered politely.
"My name is Donald. I used to live in this
house myself before I became a ghost."

Donald the Horse seemed quite nice.
Dudley was not afraid of him at all.

"So it was you making bumps in the night?"
said Dudley.
"Yes," said Donald. "And I gave you a great big
wet kiss in the dark—did you like it?"

Georgina the Ostrich and Dagmar the Baboon
liked Donald too. They thought he had pretty
eyes.

Grandpa also liked Donald. So did Trevor,
when he came to.

"Why do you haunt houses?" asked Dagmar.

"I just wanted to say hello," said Donald.
"Sometimes it gets lonely being a ghost."
Grandpa asked Donald if he liked hopscotch.
"Oh yes," said Donald. "And leapfrog too."
Trevor Hog suggested a game of leapfrog.

They were all playing leapfrog
when Madam Kreepy came out of her trance.

"Mrs. Creeper, this is our new friend, Donald,"
said Grandpa. "He used to live in this house."
Madam Kreepy shook hands with Donald.
She asked him if he liked to make fudge.
"Yes, I do," Donald said.
"But I like to make taffy better."

Donald asked his new friends if he could
visit them at night.
"Of course," they said.

Then they all played hide-and-seek.
Grandpa hid in the bathtub.
Georgina hid in the umbrella stand,
pretending her neck was an umbrella.
Donald hid under the table.

Boy, was it fun too!

By now it had stopped raining, and there was
no more thunder or lightning.
Madam Kreepy and Lazlo left as they had come,
by taxi.

The next morning Dudley found that Lazlo
had forgotten Madam Kreepy's small black bag.
Dudley looked inside it.
Besides Madam Kreepy's special hat,
he found two ham sandwiches,
a bag of gumdrops,
and a black and yellow yo-yo.

A NEW FRIEND

Donald the Horse proved a charming friend.
He often visited Dudley and his friends at night,
because ghosts can only go visiting at night.

Whenever Dudley the Stork could not sleep,
Donald would drop in for a visit.
They would color pictures together in a
coloring book, or else Donald would tell
Dudley funny stories.

Donald helped Georgina make
a pretty pink party dress.
He made taffy for Grandpa Python and
fixed Grandpa's false teeth when they broke
chewing the taffy.
He helped Trevor with his arithmetic,
and he showed Dagmar the Baboon
how to dance a jig.

And from that time on,
no one was ever
scared again at night,
even when the wind howled,
and hoot owls hooted,
and doors banged open and shut,
and things went bump in the night.

ABOUT THE AUTHOR

HARRY ALLARD was born in Evanston, Illinois. In addition to writing, he teaches French at Salem State College, in Massachusetts. His earlier books for children include *The Stupids Step Out* and *The Tutti-Frutti Case*. He now lives in Charlestown, Massachusetts.

ABOUT THE ILLUSTRATOR

JAMES MARSHALL was born and raised in San Antonio, Texas. He is the illustrator and author of the popular George and Martha books and many other favorite children's books.

It's So Nice to Have a Wolf Around the House, Allard and Marshall's earlier collaboration, was chosen as a Best Book of 1977 by both *The New York Times* and *School Library Journal*.